34X 12/03 - 11/04
40X 12/06 - 07/09
42X 1/13 (3/13)

90
86   89
11/87

Christmas

THE FAMILY CHRISTMAS TREE BOOK

CHRISTMAS
TREE
FARM

CUT YOUR OWN

The Family Christmas Tree Book

WRITTEN AND ILLUSTRATED BY
Tomie de Paola

Holiday House · New York

Library of Congress Cataloging in Publication Data

De Paola, Thomas Anthony.
  The family Christmas tree book.

  SUMMARY: A family discusses the origin of the
Christmas tree as it decorates its own.
    1. Christmas trees—Juvenile literature.
[1. Christmas trees. 2. Christmas] I. Title.
GT4989.D46   394.2'68282   80-12081
ISBN 0-8234-0416-1

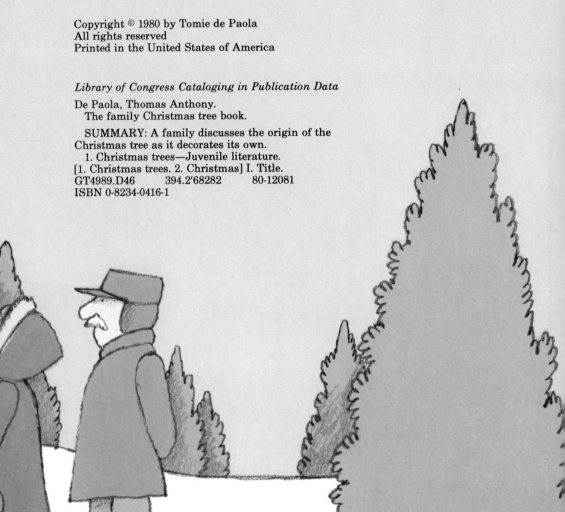

In the Middle Ages, December 24th was called Adam and Eve's Day. On that day, a play was put on in front of the churches.

Evergreen branches with apples on them were part of that play. They represented the Tree of Paradise.

I guess people liked the bright green branches, because when the medieval plays were no longer performed, people brought evergreens and even small fir trees into their homes.

Especially in Germany, they put not only apples on the trees, but also paper roses and flat wafers. The apples represented Adam and Eve; the roses, the Virgin Mary; and the wafers, the Christ Child.

These trees were called CHRISTBAUM.

Dad and I just read that in Germany, they had other Christmas things too.

One was called a PYRAMID. It was made out of wood and was decorated with branches and candles.

The other was called a LICHSTOCK, and it was a flat triangle-shaped rack just for candles.

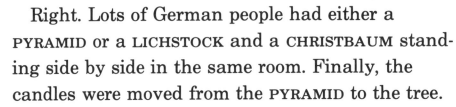

Right. Lots of German people had either a PYRAMID or a LICHSTOCK and a CHRISTBAUM standing side by side in the same room. Finally, the candles were moved from the PYRAMID to the tree.

Of course, the old-time trees were small and were put on tables. It wasn't until the Christmas tree came to America that it reached from the floor to the ceiling.

When did Christmas trees come to America?

Well, the first trees known about were decorated in 1747 by a group of people from Germany called Moravians. They lived in Bethlehem, Pennsylvania.

Little by little, as more German people moved to America, there were more Christmas trees. Other people borrowed the custom and by the 1800's many magazines had articles about them.

Famous people had Christmas trees, too. In England, Queen Victoria's German husband, Prince Albert, helped to make them popular. He gave decorated trees to schools and army barracks.

And at the palace, there was a separate tree for each of the young princes and princesses.

President Teddy Roosevelt decided not to have a Christmas tree one year, because he was worried that too many trees were being cut down. His son, Archie, was so disappointed that he decorated his own tree and hid it in a closet.

Of course, Christmas trees aren't cut down from forests any more. They are grown on "farms," like the one we went to, as a special crop.

By the 1930's, Christmas trees became really popular and now, everywhere you look at Christmastime, you'll see Christmas trees.

You know, when I was a little girl, we didn't have a Christmas tree stand. Even though they were being made, they were very expensive.

So, my father used to nail wood to the bottom of the tree. Once, we used all of my mother's flatirons to hold the tree up.

But the trees always got very dry, so one Christmas we filled a washtub with coal, put the tree in the middle of it, and added water. I remember we had to pile bricks on top of the coal, so the tree wouldn't fall over.

My mother's rich Aunt Clara had a Christmas tree stand that was a music box. As the music played, the tree went around.

There's a nice legend that a man named Martin Luther was out walking one Christmas Eve, and he saw a fir tree on a hill. It was surrounded by stars.

It looked so beautiful that he decided to surprise his family with a special Christmas tree. So, he put candles on the branches and lit them. The tree looked as though it was filled with stars.

The first electric lights were used in 1882. They were on a tree at the home of Edward Johnson. He was a friend of Thomas Edison, the man who invented the light bulb.

In 1895, Grover Cleveland was the first president to use electric lights on the tree in the White House. Each bulb had to be wired separately on the tree. Strings of lights weren't invented until 1907.

Now, there are all kinds of Christmas tree lights; little ones that glitter like stars; lights that blink on and off; lights that bubble, and even lights that look just like candles.

How come you put the lights on first, Dad?

Did any of you know that almost all glass ornaments used to come from one village in Germany called LAUSCHA?

They were all made by hand.

American businessmen, including Mr. Woolworth, began importing them and, by 1930, 95% of all glass ornaments hanging on American Christmas trees came from this village.

It wasn't until 1939 that glass ornaments were made in America.

There are so many different ways to decorate a Christmas tree.

The main thing is that every family's Christmas tree is very special to that family.

Ready?

FIGURE A

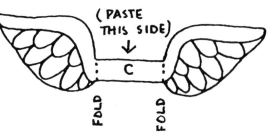

(PASTE THIS SIDE)

C

FOLD   FOLD

FIGURE B

A Make-It-Yourself Angel Ornament

IMPORTANT:
Do not cut the decoration from this book.

   1. Trace the angel (Figure A) and the wings (Figure B) on heavier paper.

   2. Color the angel any way you wish. Also, color Part A and the front and back of the wings.

   3. Carefully cut out the angel and the wings.

   4. Fold the "fold-lines" towards the back.

   5. Tape or paste Part A on top of Part B.

   6. Tape or paste the wings to the angel by matching the C's. Bend the wings.

   7. Double a string or heavy thread and push the loop through the hole at the top. Knot the ends together.

   8. Hang on your tree.

⑦